TRUE FACES

A CIARA STEELE NOVELLA, #1

CATHERINE BANKS

TURBO KITTEN

Avery, thank you for supporting me and believing in me.

ACKNOWLEDGMENTS

This book would not have been possible without the support of my husband and family. Thank you.

Thank you MerryBookRound for creating such gorgeous covers.

Thank you to my editors.

And thank you, as always, to my fans.

TRUE FACES

USA Today Bestselling Author

CATHERINE BANKS

A CIARA STEELE
NOVELLA, #1

PROLOGUE

I hated sitting in the tree outside of her window, watching her like some sick perverted stalker, but I couldn't stand having her out of my sight. Her buttery skin and blonde hair blended perfectly with her hazel eyes that changed from blue to green when she was upset and speckled with brown when she was frightened. She was one of the few women left who were skinny, but built with an hour glass shape. Her shape begged me to run my hands along it and trace the curves.

I watched as she practiced kickboxing with her radio blaring heavy metal rock music. Sweat trickled down her chest and disappeared in to her tank top between her average sized, but perfectly proportioned breasts. She was perfect and I wanted her. The others would sense the difference in her soon and I had to claim her before they tried to take her. But the women of this century are much different than those of past ones. And this woman is more different than any other of her century.

I love her and she doesn't even know I exist.

Such a cruel world.

ONE

Akio flicked the center of my forehead making me cringe in pain. "Still open," He grunted. Akio was short, Chinese and very powerful. He could kick my butt in two seconds even though he was very very old.

I groaned and continued my Qigong movements and tried to focus on the center of my forehead.

"I don't understand why I can't just focus on closing the eye first and then do the other training." I complained.

"I teacher. You student. Now focus." Akio flicked my forehead again making me wince in pain.

I sighed, but continued with the lesson. Akio raised his fingers toward my forehead after two minutes of watching me, but I grabbed his wrist before he could hit the center of my forehead where my invisible, but very real, third eye sat.

"Anymore and I'll be blind instead of being able to close the third eye," I whispered calmly.

Akio frowned at me, his deep wrinkles deepening further. I fought to push back the image of the dragon that was overlapping his face.

"Fine. No more today, but you must practice," he said angrily.

I put my right palm over my left fist and bowed to Akio. "Thank you Master." He nodded once and hobbled toward the back of the dojo where his living quarters were. I changed quickly into my work clothes then slung my backpack over my shoulders and walked down the busy city street. The sun dried the sweat on my face as I walked toward one of the seven skyscrapers in the city.

Luna Villa was a two horse town when Akio purchased his property in sixteen thirty four, but in the eighteen hundreds the werewolf superstition spread and tourists swarmed to any city they believed could house wolves. What better place to look for werewolves than the "moon village"?

Tourism was still booming three hundred years later and the merchandisers milked them for all they could. You could get a mug, a shirt, even a blanket with a picture of a half man, half wolf beast howling at the moon. The drawings were laughable and I knew the real werewolves despised the drawings. Yes, I said real werewolves. Not a very nice group to socialize with, but they seemed to like it in Luna Villa since hundreds of werewolves lived in the town. There were many other preternaturals living in Luna Villa as well and it made for a very frightening place to be out at night in.

The normal humans had no idea and the werewolves played it up around the full moon, running through town in their wolf forms or in combatant form (half man-half wolf). The tourists would run to the cops and tell them how their friend was eaten by a werewolf and the cops would shoo them away as drunk and needing to get their fantasies in check with reality. Sadly, it was the cops who needed a check in reality.

I stopped at the red crosswalk sign and waited for the little white man to signal me to walk.

Two men stopped beside me and the hair on the nape of my neck stood up. I turned my head slowly and my eyes widened. Over the men's human faces flickered images of two ogres who were smiling at me, revealing decaying brown teeth. I turned away quickly and stared straight ahead trying to act like I had no idea they were ogres and favored the taste of human flesh.

The signal finally changed and I walked quickly across the street. I couldn't run or they would know I could see their true faces. I made it two more blocks without seeing another preternatural until a werelion stepped in front of me smiling wide. The blurred image of his razor sharp teeth overlapped the small human ones and would have made me scream if I wasn't used to seeing it every day. "Hey girl. You look like you could use a good time."

I swallowed the lump in my throat and shook my head. "Sorry, I'm taken," I said as strongly as I could. His nostrils flared and I knew I was sunk. He wouldn't smell a man on me and would press the issue. It was broad daylight dammit. They usually didn't pull stunts like this until night.

He flared his nostrils again, looked behind me then shrugged and stepped out of my way. "My bad."

I wanted to look behind me to see what he had seen, but knew that something that would have frightened a werelion would have probably made me wet my pants. I walked quickly away from him and started counting down the blocks to my work.

Five.

Four.

Three.

Two.

One.

I opened the front door and hurried inside flashing my security badge at the guard as I ran past. I turned toward the front door as I waited for the elevator and crossed my fingers. The elevator dinged and no monsters followed me inside. Thank goodness. I climbed into my metal safe haven and pressed the button for the sixth floor. Preternaturals hate to be in confined spaces so the elevator was the only safe place for me at work, but sometimes they used the elevator and I was forced to share the box with them.

I slowed my breathing down and whispered, "As long as the monsters don't know I can see them, they won't hurt me." If only it were true and I believed it.

The elevator doors opened and the noise of the office brought a smile to my face. Secretaries, running between their desks and their attorneys' offices, yelled orders to clerks. Attorneys yelled orders at the secretaries and yelled insults at the other attorneys. The phones constantly rung and music from the employee jukebox filled the air with a static hum. I loved my job.

After grabbing a cup of coffee and adding two sugars and one cream, I rushed to Robert's office. He was yelling at the phone, so I knocked on the door and stood just outside of it. He slammed the phone receiver down and motioned me in. "Morning sir," I said with a pleasant smile on my face.

He nodded at me shaking around his grey hair and pointed to a stack of tapes and files. "I need all of the letters and legal pleadings out today and I need coffee."

I set the coffee on his desk and picked up the files and tapes. "Right away. Remember, you have a deposition in conference room four in two hours and a counselors meeting at three in the executive conference room on the first floor."

Robert rubbed his temples. "What is the point of a counselors meeting? The chief will tell us we're doing a great job, the other attorneys will gloat about recent wins and then a debate will ensue which won't get finished because no one can agree on anything. It's absurd."

I smiled. "And you love every second of it."

He started to smile then shook his head and frowned. "Coffee, now." Any other secretary would have objected that she'd just gotten him a cup of coffee, but I knew he would chug the first cup and would need the second one by the time I got back to him.

I turned and left his office before he could think of some way to make me go to the counselors meeting in his place. I set the files and tapes on my desk and put my backpack in the bottom drawer. Sally popped her head up over the cubicle wall and smiled at me. "So, did you meet anyone?"

I rolled my eyes at her and pushed her red-haired head back over the wall. "I stayed home all weekend and watched episodes of Buffy." We both sat down before one of the attorneys saw us talking and docked our pay.

Sally sighed. "I don't understand your infatuation with that teen vampire show."

"Vampire *slayer* show," I corrected her. "And there is nothing wrong with Buffy. Wouldn't you enjoy slaying a few demons?"

Sally replied without hesitation, "I'd settle for a few attorneys."

I laughed quietly and hurried away from my desk towards the full kitchen. The attorneys spent more time at work than at home, so they decided to put in a full kitchen where they could make their secretaries cook them food. Three other secretaries I had never seen before were pouring coffee and tea into mugs for their attorneys when I stepped into the kitchen. I waited my turn for the caffeinated pot of coffee then grabbed Robert's favorite mug sporting a penguin with a green tie asking, "What do you mean it doesn't match my suit?" and poured the coffee in.

I started adding sugar when one of the secretaries started talking to me. I stirred the liquid and smiled politely. "Sorry I didn't hear your question?"

She was a thin woman, almost too thin. It made me wonder if a kick to her side would break a rib. "I asked if you had seen the new attorney or if you knew who was assigned to him?" She asked with a bright smile.

I frowned. "I didn't know there was a new attorney." Sally always kept me up to date on office gossip. Had she forgotten to tell me or was she holding out on me?

One of the other secretaries, a woman too obese for her tight shirt, rolled her eyes. "I don't know how you could have missed him. He's only got the most perfect brown eyes and black hair I have ever seen."

The last secretary, the type of woman who tended to be overlooked no matter what she was wearing, groaned. "And the most luscious body." All three women giggled loudly like teenage girls.

I washed off the spoon I had used to stir Robert's coffee and shrugged. "Well I hope one of you gets assigned to him." They waved and I hurried to Robert's office. I didn't really care about new attorneys and office gossip, but I preferred to be kept in the loop so that I didn't look like an idiot when someone asked me a question about what had happened recently.

A hot attorney would at least be something to look at instead of these other, old attorneys that worked here. We did have one younger attorney, but he was not attractive.

I walked into Robert's office and set his mug in front of him and was almost out the door when he called my name. I winced and turned around slowly. "Yes, sir?"

He had on his serious frown, the one that meant he was upset. "The chief has informed me that you're being reassigned."

My mouth dropped open. "But...but I'm always here. I'm never late and I get your work out on time. Did I misspell something or not check a box?"

Robert waved his hand to stop me. "Calm down, Ciara. You didn't do anything wrong. You're being promoted."

I closed my mouth then asked, "What floor?"

He smiled. "First."

I sighed. Dammit. That was the floor where the monsters worked, but it was also the Executive members. "Which attorney is it?"

He straightened his tie, a sign that he felt threatened by this new attorney. "The new hot shot, Eric Wolfe."

"Wolf?" My voice picked up a few octaves.

Robert sighed and placed his hands on his desk. "Ciara, I don't have much time. Yes, you're Eric Wolfe's new secretary. He's already left for the day so the Chief told me to have you pack your stuff and set up your desk by Wolfe's office and then go home. *I don't see why he gets to miss the counselors meeting.*"

I recomposed myself and smiled. "It's been a pleasure working with you, Robert."

Robert nodded and picked up his ringing phone. I shut his door and walked numbly to my desk. Sally walked around her cubicle to stand by me. "What's up? You look like you got docked money again."

I shook my head. "I got a promotion."

She smiled. "That's great! Where are you going?"

I pointed down. "First floor. New attorney."

She gasped and lowered her voice. "You got Wolfe?! You bitch!"

I frowned and looked up at her. "What?"

"He's got to be one of the sexiest lawyers practicing. I was hoping to get that job, but you do deserve a raise."

I smiled. "A raise? Hmm, maybe this won't be so bad."

She rolled her eyes. "You are a piece of work, Ciara. Only you would act devastated about getting a promotion." She looked at the files and tapes piled on my desk. "Let me guess, these are rushes for today?"

I smiled. "Yeah."

She sighed. "Hand 'em over. I'll divvy them out." I handed her the stack then started packing up my personal belongings, which consisted of a calendar with forest pictures that Akio had purchased for me, a samurai bobblehead and my back-pack. I walked to the elevator and took a steadying breath. Down to first floor hell I go. The raise had better be worth looking at preternaturals all day.

The elevator dinged loudly at the bottom floor sounding like a bell in my head. I walked out and toward the ornate double doors that led to the executive area. I opened the doors and froze as every set of eyes turned toward me. Every single employee was a preternatural. Shit. I walked to the head secretary and smiled as best as I could manage. "I'm Ciara Steele."

She nodded and pointed straight. "Eric Wolfe, office one

thirty." I walked past all of the silent workers as they followed me with their eyes and hurried into my new office.

I have my own office! I closed my door and heard averagely loud work noise start up. It was too quiet down here. No yelling, no music and no phones ringing more than once. I set my bobble head on top of my new flat screen computer monitor and hung my calendar on the wall. I looked around my office and smiled. Two of the walls were solid and two were glass. The glass wall to the right faced Mr. Wolfe's office and the wall in front of me faced the walkway to my office. My office was a portal from the normal workers to his office. It was designed that way so that I could keep the nuisances away from the attorney. I knew this because I had come here after hours out of curiosity and talked with a secretary who was working late.

He must be really good to be new and get this office. I opened the door to his office and peeked inside. Solid walls all the way around except for the one into my office. He could see me and I could see him, but no one else could see him. Complete privacy for him and partial privacy for me. I shut his door and grabbed my backpack. That was when I noticed a small yellow note on my keyboard. It was a sticky note with elegant writing on it. I picked it up and stared in shock at the note.

"Can't wait to begin our relationship.
I know we'll make a great team.

~Eric W."

None of the attorneys at the firm had ever written me a nice note before. Maybe he wouldn't be so bad? I put the note on the bottom corner of my computer and smiled. I could handle a group of preternatural secretaries and attorneys. I walked to the head secretary and asked, "Are there any forms I need to fill out?"

She shook her head and handed me a piece of paper. "Here's your new salary statement. Mr. W wants you here at seven thirty tomorrow morning. Don't be late."

I looked at the salary and gasped. "A...are you sure this is the right one?"

She frowned at me, her long canine ears flattening to her head. "I don't make mistakes."

I swallowed nervously. "Of course not. My apology." I hurried out of the double doors and out of the building. I let the sun warm my cold skin and looked at the salary again. "Seventy five *thousand* dollars?! Shopping spree here I come!" I yelled excitedly. I folded the paper and put it inside my backpack before jogging down the sidewalk. I danced nervously from foot to foot as I waited at the crosswalk for the signal to change and charged across smiling at the wereanimals and fairies in human disguises walking by me. I opened the door to The Office, the clothing store that the top executives purchased their clothes from, and smiled at the saleswoman. "I need a new set of clothes."

She smiled at me politely. "What position?"

I pulled out my salary statement. "Executive Assistant to a level four attorney."

Her mouth dropped a little before she recovered and smiled. "Right this way, Ma'am."

TWO

Three hours of shopping later and my arms were loaded with packages. The saleswoman flagged down a taxi for me and even paid my fare. Being promoted was definitely a great way to start the day. The cabbie dropped me off on the outskirts of town where I lived, pressed against the forest and helped me to the door of my house. I thanked him and hurried inside, shutting the door and locking all three deadbolts.

I ran up the stairs and emptied my shopping bags on to my bed. I giggled in delight and held a black pinstriped dress up in front of me so I could look at it in the mirror. "Hmm... maybe next week." I hung the dress up and then held a pantsuit outfit up to my body in front of the mirror. It hugged all the right curves and was very classy. "We have a winner." I hung the outfit on the mirror and started hanging the rest of the clothes up in the closet then finished by sorting the shoes, socks, hosiery and underwear.

I skipped down the stairs and turned on the stereo, sighing happily as Metallica slammed in to my eardrums. Preternaturals hate loud noises, so I prefer them. I kicked my shoes off and swung my head around as I skipped to the kitchen. My house was two stories and pretty large for only me to live in, but my parents had left it to me in their will and so I treasured it.

I opened the fridge and took out the leftover pasta from last night and stuck it in the microwave, dancing in place while I watched the timer countdown. The hair on the nape of my neck stood up and fear crept over my skin. I spun around and stared out the window. Nothing, at least nothing that I could see. "Damn, I'm getting too paranoid," I whispered. I took out the pasta, grabbed a soda, checked all of the locks on the doors and windows and ran up the stairs to my room. I turned on the television to the news channel while I ate my dinner.

After finishing my dinner, I stretched in the center of my room. I only had a full-length mirror, dresser, bed and television in my room so that I could have enough room to practice my kickboxing, pilates, yoga, and Qigong. I took a cleansing breath and started my Qigong, watching the television and trying to close my other sight. I was born with my third eye open allowing me to see people's real faces. It's not a physical third eye, that makes me look like a freak, but a metaphysical eye that allows me to see more than any other human. The open third eye means that no glamour can hide the monsters from my sight. It's horrible. It makes it very hard to talk to preternatural because I usually end up staring at their non-human parts and inevitably insult them even though they don't know I can see them.

I want to be able to close the third eye and lead a normal life without seeing fangs, wings and phantom body parts. Every day I am in danger and I know it, but until I close it I cannot do anything about it. If anyone found out about my ability I could be killed or tortured or whatever they decided was a fitting punishment for being able to see them. My parents freaked when they found out about my ability and dropped me off at Akio's when I was six. Akio and I have been working since then to close my eye, but I haven't been able to. The damn thing is determined to stay open. Nevertheless, I continue to try.

I closed my eyes, took a deep breath and went through my movements. I looked at the television and saw the reporter. She was an attractive Asian woman, except for the horns growing out of her head. I focused on the center of my forehead where the eye was and imagined closing it. The horns wavered and then came in to better focus. "Dammit!" I yelled.

I exhaled and tried again, this time focusing on a satyr in the background. His hooves faded then...disappeared! "Yes!" I looked back at the reporter and screamed in joy. She looked human. "Yes! YES! YEEEESSSSSS!!!!!! Finally!" I laughed in joy and ran downstairs and out the front door, not bothering to lock it in my excitement. I ran as fast as I could down the sidewalk ignoring the bewildered stares of those I ran by. I ran up the steps of the dojo and flung open the door. "AKIO!!!!!"

Akio opened the door to his bedroom, which was adjoined to the dojo. "What is it? Are you hurt?" He asked as he hobbled towards me.

I ran to him and hugged him tightly. "It's closed! I closed the third eye! I can't see your other faces!"

Akio's eyes widened in shock. "Closed? Completely?"

I nodded. "I did it, Akio. Finally, after all of these years I closed it."

Akio frowned. "Open it."

I stared at him in shock. "What?"

15

"Open it," He said again.

I stepped back from him. "No. No Akio I just closed it. What if I can't do it again?

He glared at me. "What if you can't open it again?"

I raised my voice at Akio for the first time in my life. "Good! I hope it never opens again!"

He shook his head, "You must open it. You must be able to control it, not lose your ability. Now open it!"

I shook my head and walked backwards away from him. "I thought you would be happy for me? I closed it and am normal now."

Akio sighed. "You will never be normal, Ciara. You are a Seer and you must open your eye. What if a prophecy comes and you cannot see it? We must train you to close and open. Not just one. It is dangerous to keep it closed."

I gaped at him. "Dangerous? It's dangerous to have it open. You know that as well as I do. No, I won't open it." I turned my back on Akio.

Akio spoke softly. "You will understand, Ciara. You will need it open. Come back when you are not being so childish."

I fought the urge to yell and ran out of the dojo and back to my house. Tears stung my eyes and wet my cheeks. I ran into my house and locked the door. He was wrong. I knew it. I would not open the eye. I climbed up the stairs and into bed and closed my eyes.

THREE

The alarm blared rock music in my ear, making me sit up in bed. I slowed my breathing and turned the alarm off. My first day of work at my new position was today. I hurried through my morning routine so I could spend extra time on my makeup and hair so I would look perfect for my new boss. Once I felt that I looked decent enough, I grabbed my backpack and started my walk to work. I looked at everyone's face and smiled. All human looking! My eye was still closed. I walked a little faster and walked in the front doors of the building at seven ten. The guard nodded at me and I opened the doors to the executive office. Only two other secretaries were in and both looked human. I smiled wide and walked confidently to my new office. I stopped in the doorway and stared at a man placing flowers on my desk. He turned around after setting them down and smiled at me. "Oh, you're early. I was hoping to have these here when you came in."

He wasn't handsome, he was a god. His black hair was cut short and his golden-brown eyes seemed to be looking into my soul. His wide jaw was strong and his shoulders wide. His suit hid all his muscles but I could tell he was much bigger than an average man. He had to work out often, but the best thing was that there were no other faces, just his. I realized I was staring at him and not speaking and cleared my throat. "Thank you for the flowers. It's very thoughtful."

He reached down and picked my hand up. "One can never be too kind to a lady." I watched in amazement as he kissed the back of my hand. His lips were warm and soft against my hand. "I am looking forward to working with you, Ciara."

I swallowed the drool threatening to leak out of my mouth and nodded. "I hope I can meet your expectations."

He released my hand and smiled. "I'm sure you will surpass all of my expectations." I shivered at the multiple meanings behind his sentence. "Get settled then come into my office and we'll go over my calendar and your things."

I nodded as I set my backpack down, turned away from his office and took a cleansing breath. I had to get my hormones in check. He was my boss and you do not date the boss. I took another breath then turned and knocked on his door. "Come in," he said softly. I walked into his office and smiled professionally. He smiled back sitting in his large executive leather chair behind his large marble desk. "And you don't ever need to knock. You are always welcome in here."

That was a first. Most attorneys preferred their privacy and would yell at you if you came in without knocking. I nodded and sat down in one of the guest chairs that matched his desk. He opened a briefcase and took out two phones and two leather calendars and set them on the desk. "I don't know how they operate upstairs, but in executive we must be coordinated with our assistants. So, this phone and calendar are for you. I have already programmed my numbers and events in them for you."

I took the phone and calendar and stared at them in shock. "Thank you, Mr. Wolfe." It was the nicest thing anyone had ever done for me.

He looked at me seriously. "Call me, Eric. I gave you my work numbers and personal numbers. If there is ever anything you need you can call me anytime. No matter how small it is or if its work related or not. I want us to be friends as well as partners."

I frowned. "Partners?"

He nodded and folded his hands across the desk and stared into my eyes. I found that I could not look away and was forced to stare into the deep depths of them. What was it about them that made me feel like he could see into my soul? "We have to be a team. It would never work if I just treated you as my secretary. I don't want you to think of me as your boss. I don't want you think that you can't talk to me about anything. I want you to be able to come to me about anything and me be able to speak to you about everything." He glanced down at his Rolex and sighed. "I've got to go to the counselors meeting. They postponed it just so I could attend."

I smiled. "How thoughtful of them."

He rolled his eyes. "Right. I don't have anything for you to do right now since I'm still reviewing my new files so you could just play with your new phone and if there are any days you would like off you can put them on the phone's calendar and they will automatically be added to mine."

I frowned. "There aren't any days I'll need off."

He smiled. "There must be some days. Family events or boyfriend's birthdays?"

I shook my head. "No. My work is my family. I have no... I'm not involved with anyone so it won't be a problem." I said the last with a smile, trying to play good secretary even though I felt the sadness stirring within me. It had been a long time since I had said it out loud.

His face turned serious, but I could see a sparkle in his eyes. "Oh. Well, if there are any days that come up don't be afraid to ask."

"Thank you, but I doubt that." I picked up the phone and calendar and walked to my office. I sat down and turned on my computer and flicked the samurai bobble head.

Eric walked into my office and straightened his tie. "How do I look? Do I look brilliant and tough?"

I nodded. "Yes Mister...I mean Eric. You look brilliant and tough." *And sexy.*

He nodded and walked out of my office, closing the door behind him. I put a hand up to my face and sighed. I was blushing. Dammit. So much for being professional on the first day. I logged into my computer than played with the settings on my new phone. I tried to pass the hours by with my new gadget, but with no typing to do I was bored. Eric finally came back four hours later and slumped against my door. "That was fun." He loosened his tie and walked into his office leaving the door open. "Have you ever been to one of those meetings before?" He asked from inside his office.

I stood up and walked to stand in his doorway. "No. They don't allow secretaries in."

He frowned. "I think I'm going to have to change that so that someone can intervene. Four hours of nothing. Just old men complaining about old things. What a waste of time. Did I get any calls?"

I shook my head. "None."

He smiled. "Well you're probably bored. How about I take you out for lunch?"

I stared at him in shock. "Um, Eric I don't..."

He frowned and then smiled. "Of course. I understand. It might not look right if the new attorney takes his newly promoted secretary out to lunch. It's alright. Rain check for a later date?"

I nodded. "Sure."

He stretched his arms up over his head and I couldn't help but wonder what his stomach looked like. Did he have a flat stomach or was it a six pack? I shook my head and he smiled. "How about you take the rest of the day off?"

I smiled back at him. "That's very generous of you, but..."

He shook his head. "Go on. There's nothing for you to do here yet. I'll see you tomorrow morning at seven thirty. I've got a deposition at ten and I'll need you to start on Substitutions of Attorney for the files I'm taking over. So, we'll start the real work tomorrow."

A nice attorney. Wow. And I thought those were just fairy tales. "Thank you Mister...I mean Eric."

His phone started ringing and he sighed. "Now you better hurry before I get something for you to do. See you tomorrow." I turned to leave and his voice stopped me. "And Ciara... stay safe."

I frowned. "Uh, sure. See you tomorrow." He picked up the phone and started arguing with the caller. I hurried out of his office, shutting his door quietly and grabbed my new calendar and phone and put them in my backpack before hurrying out of the office. A paid day out of the office again. I had better use the time while I could. Unlike the previous day I walked slowly out of the office and stood casually as I waited for the signal to change. It was incredible not to see the scary faces of the preternaturals and I felt an incredible weight gone from my shoulders. I made my necessary stop at the grocery store and then flagged down a taxi to my house.

After I was sure I had locked all of the doors and all of the windows were still locked I started cooking lunch and dinner for the day. Even though I had a raise I knew I needed to keep my spending down so that I didn't end up broke. I really didn't want to end up eating noodles for a month like I had last year. The kitchen had all of the necessities I needed and would need if I had a family of six. An hour later I had baked a lasagna and the smell filled the kitchen. I spooned out my lunch portion of the lasagna I had just finished cooking and then packed the rest in plastic containers to eat later. I sat down on my leather couch and turned the television on to the cartoon channel.

No, there is nothing wrong with a twenty-two-year-old watching cartoons. I'm always referred to as a young adult so acting young is perfectly okay. The hours passed by slowly and dinner was just as boring. I cleaned the dishes then went to my room to read until I fell asleep. I realized as I grabbed the book, which I was currently reading, that I led a very boring life. Without my training with Akio I didn't have anything to do or anyone to spend time with. I made a decision to start going out and live life before I turned into the crazy cat lady. I needed a boyfriend or at least someone I could go out with.

Eric's face flashed in front of my eyes and I shook my head. I couldn't date my boss. Not only would that end badly for my career it would kill my self esteem when he said no. Plus it wasn't likely that he didn't have a wife or girlfriend already.

After reading for a few hours my eyelids grew heavy and I could finally sleep. I curled up under my blankets and dreamed of a life without preternaturals.

The next few days went by slowly and normally. Eric gave

me letters to type and I assisted him at some of his depositions all without seeing any preternatural faces looking back at me. Eric was the nicest attorney I had met and one day while we were on a lunch break from a deposition, I asked him, "Are you human?"

His smile faltered slightly and he asked, "What do you mean am I human?"

I shrugged. "It's just that I haven't met an attorney like you before. Usually all of the high-powered attorneys aren't..."

Eric laughed. "Well I'm sure you'll see me at a trial and take back that comment. I believe that in order to be an attorney you have to channel the beast within."

I stared at my plate in shock for a second. The phrase he had just used was part of the wereanimals mantra. I closed my eyes and focused my attention on my third eye. I prayed it would open so I could see if Eric was in fact human as I thought. I opened my eyes and looked at him, but only saw his handsome face smiling at me. I looked to the right and left and still only saw human faces. Damn. Maybe I would have to go back to Akio to have him train me. Maybe he was right. Was it in fact safer for me to be able to open it and see if the people around me were preternaturals and possibly dangerous for me?

Eric sipped his water and watched me. "Are you feeling alright?"

I took a swig from my cup and nodded. "I just realized that my teacher might have been right and I hate it when I'm wrong."

"Your teacher? So, you take college classes?" He asked.

I shook my head. "No, he's my sensei. I take classes at a dojo."

He leaned back. "See, this is what I want. I want to know

more about you. If we are going to make a great team, we have to know about each other."

I shrugged. "There really isn't much to know about me. I occasionally take lessons at the dojo near my house, read books and go to work."

His eyes were sparkling with interest. "Do you own or rent?"

I found myself mesmerized by his voice and face and instantly answered his question. "Own."

"Do you have any animals?"

I shook my head. "My circumstances don't permit animals."

He frowned. "What circumstances?"

I closed my eyes and the trance was gone. Was he using some type of power on me? I felt the warmth in my stomach and sighed. Hormones. Damn. "What about you, Eric? There must be a Mrs. Wolfe or a future Mrs. Wolfe."

He frowned deeper for a second then shook his head and smiled. "No, I haven't found a woman that I've felt is right for me."

I stared at him in shock for a second. He was single. I cleared my throat. "So, do you live in town?"

He shook his head. "I live about ten minutes down the highway off of the old post trail."

I nodded, knowing where he was talking about. "Out in the forest, right? My house is on the other side of the forest."

He smiled. "So, we're neighbors then? Who would have known?"

I asked the one question I had been dying to know, "How old are you?"

He asked, "How old do you think I am?" with a sexy smile.

I rolled my eyes. "You can't answer a question with a question."

He laughed. "Twenty-six. And you?"

I smiled. "Twenty-two." I looked down at my PDA and sighed. "Time to get back."

Eric groaned. "Are you sure you couldn't fake a seizure or something so we could get out of this? I have a feeling this deposition is going to take multiple days to finish."

I smiled. "Better to get it done now then save it for later. You do have a trial coming up in a few weeks. It would be murder for you to have to work on a deposition while preparing for trial."

Eric nodded and stood up. "You're right. See, I knew we'd make a great team."

I smiled and followed him out of the restaurant and to the building where the deposition was taking place. The deponent was a short, angry man who reminded me of a mountain dwarf. In fact, I was positive that if I could See him that that was what he was. We sat down around the large table and Eric began questioning the man again. Another two hours into the questioning and the man started getting angry. He was fidgeting and his face was blushed. I tried to signal Eric, but he was too engrossed in the questions. The man looked right at me and asked, "Can you See me?"

My eyes widened and I looked at Eric who shook his head. Eric spoke quiet but firm. "Mr. Wallace, I would ask that you refrain from speaking to my assistant. In this deposition I will ask the questions and you will answer. Do you understand?"

Mr. Wallace ignored Eric and bared his teeth at me. "You know. You're a Seer!" He jumped across the table and grabbed me by the throat and pulled me out of my chair. For such a little man he was very strong.

Eric rose from his chair slowly and I could see the worry and anger in his face. "Mr. Wallace, release my assistant."

Mr. Wallace shook his head and took a step back, pulling me with him. "I won't go back to the weres. I won't work for them again."

I tensed. Weres? He had to mean wereanimals. If he was afraid of going to wereanimals then he would do anything he had to, including kill me. I looked up at Eric and noticed his hands were balled in to fists at his side. "Release her or the weres or whatever you are talking about will be the least of your worries."

Mr. Wallace moved his lower hand and then a knife appeared at my throat. Shit. I really hated magic some days. I grabbed the arm with the knife, squatted down and tossed Mr. Wallace over my head. When I looked up Eric was already pinning him to the floor and securing his hands with zip ties. A guard came in to the room and carried the unconscious dwarf out of the room. Eric rushed over to me and ran his hand along my throat. "Are you alright?"

His hand was extremely warm and soothing to the scratch I had gotten from the knife. I looked up into his concerned eyes and nodded. "I'm fine. The knife scratched my skin when I threw him, but didn't draw blood."

Eric helped me stand up, but put his arm around my waist as though he thought I would faint. "That was very brave of you to do that, but I would ask that you never do something like that again."

I realized I was leaning against him and it wasn't because I needed the support. I pulled away from his arms and smiled. "I guess the depo is over?"

Eric smiled. "Yes." He turned to the court reporter and recapped the events in words for the record, then started packing his briefcase. I helped him put everything away and grabbed my own documents and notes before following Eric out of the room and out of the building's doors. Eric stayed silent until we got into his blue 2010 Nissan Skyline and closed the doors. "Are you sure that you're alright? Would you like to take the rest of the day off?"

I looked at Eric's body and face and sighed. He was tense, like a coiled snake ready to spring. "I'm fine. The scratch on my neck isn't even bleeding. It's not your fault Eric."

He gripped the steering wheel and I heard the leather creak in protest. "I would not have been able to forgive myself if he had hurt you."

I reached out slowly and rested my hand on one of his. "You couldn't have stopped him and it wasn't your fault that he snapped." Actually, it was mine. Somehow, he knew that I was a Seer. How when I didn't actually even See him?

Eric looked at me and I swore his eyes had a brighter golden tint to them than usual. "I could have done something," he whispered. He started the car and we drove in silence to the office. Eric stayed in his office with the blinds drawn and the door closed the rest of the afternoon. I tried to focus on my work, but I couldn't stop thinking about the way he said he could have done something. Was he just upset that he hadn't been able to help me? Was it a natural human response or was there some underlying meaning? When it was finally time to go home, I knocked twice on the door, then peeked my head into his office. Eric was staring at a picture of a forest on his wall silently. "Eric, I'm leaving."

He spun around in his chair and his eyes grew wide. "Leaving?"

I smiled. "It's six."

He exhaled with a hand on his heart. "Oh, I thought you meant *leaving*. Alright, have a good weekend."

I nodded. "You too. And Eric?"

He looked back up at me from his desk. "Hmm?"

I smiled. "Fighting always relieves my anger. You might want to think about joining a dojo."

He laughed and waved. "I'll see you on Monday."

I closed his door and grabbed my backpack. I had promised myself that I would go out tonight so I hurried home to shower and change. I glared at my reflection for thirty minutes after I was ready and tried to figure out what I could change. Nothing came to mind so I stuffed my cash, ID and credit card in my pocket and headed down the street to one of the three dance clubs in town. I showed the bouncer my ID and made my way through the crowd to the bar. The bartender was muscled, tattooed and only wearing a pair of pants. He smiled seductively at me. "What'll it be?"

I smiled back at him. "Two shots of whiskey." He poured the shots and I handed him my cash, smiling at him when he purposefully touched my hand when getting the cash. I exhaled and downed the two shots one right after the other. The liquor burned down my throat and warmed my stomach.

The music changed to a techno song and I maneuvered my way to the middle of the dance floor and started dancing. An attractive man in his late thirties started dancing with me and I decided to let him instead of turning him away. He wouldn't be my pick for the night, but I didn't want to be rude. When the song ended, I moved to another part of the dance floor and within seconds a man in his mid twenties, who was very attractive, started dancing with me. Akio and some of the other students had always insisted I was very attractive, but when I looked at myself, I only saw the flaws. I couldn't deny that I did draw attention when I went out though.

The man moved closer to me and asked, "What's your name?"

I put my lips against his ear and said, "Ciara and I need a drink."

He smiled. "I'm Nate." I followed Nate to the bar and ordered two more shots. Nate raised an eyebrow, but said nothing. Nate took his shot and I took my two and led him back out onto the dance floor. The song changed to a fast tempo techno remake and I moved my hips in a figure eight faster and faster in front of Nate. He moved closer to me and then pressed his hips against mine and matched my movements perfectly and gracefully. Shit, he was a preternatural. I tried to pull away, but he wrapped his arm around my waist and pressed his groin against my butt. He was *very* happy to see me.

I tried to pull away again, but he held me tight and whispered in my ear, "Don't be afraid, Seer. I'm very generous in the bedroom."

I ripped away from him and ran face first in to Eric's muscular chest. "Eric? What are you doing here?" I asked in shock.

Eric ignored me and glared at Nate. "You should be more polite to women."

Nate's lips raised in what I assumed was supposed to be a smile, but looked more like baring his teeth. "I didn't know you were in town, Eric."

Eric rested his hand on my shoulder and gave Nate the same type of smile. "Now you do."

Nate looked at Eric's hand on my shoulder and scoffed. "So, not worth it."

Eric watched him walk away then pulled his hand away. I felt cold where his warm hand had just been. "Are you okay? Did he hurt you?"

I rolled my eyes and felt the liquor kicking in. "I'm fine. Jeez. And you didn't answer my question."

Eric smiled. "I come here every weekend."

Of course, I had to pick the club that he came to. "Well I'll just leave then."

Eric grabbed my arm and stopped me from walking away. "I thought we were friends, Ciara?"

His hand warmed my cold arm and I instantly imagined how warm it would be to have his naked body pressed against mine. "We are, but I don't want to intrude on your night. You only get three nights away from me. I don't want you to feel obligated to be around me just because we work together," I said.

Eric tilted my chin up with his hand and I realized I was leaning in to his palm. "I like being around you."

I pulled away from him and swallowed. "I think I need another drink."

Eric frowned. "You sure? I think you might have had enough."

I glared at him then stormed to the bar. "Two shots." The bartender looked at Eric and then hurriedly filled the shot glasses. I took one shot then reached for the other, but Eric grabbed it. "That's mine." I said irritably.

Eric sniffed it then coughed. "I don't understand how you can drink this."

I slammed the shot then shivered as the liquor spread in my stomach. "It's the only thing I've found that can warm me." Eric stared at me in shock, but didn't say anything. The song changed to one of my favorites and I smiled. "Gotta dance." I spun onto the dance floor and started dancing. I hadn't realized Eric was still there until I spun a little too fast and he caught me before I fell. I blushed. "Sorry."

He put my arms around his neck and his hands on my lower back just above my butt. "No apology necessary." He danced well for a man and I found myself smiling at him and enjoying the feel of his hands on me. My fingers moved up the back of his neck and found his hair. It was thicker than any I had ever felt and yet still incredibly silky soft. I jumped back from him and stumbled, landing on my butt. He reached down to help me up and I backed away from him. "I...you're my boss."

He helped me stand up and frowned. "You can't dance with me because I'm your boss?"

I backed away from him and hurried through the crowd to the bartender. "Whiskey."

Eric stepped up next to me and shook his head at the bartender. "I think you've had enough."

I wanted to yell at him, but didn't want to make him angry. I hopped onto the bar on my stomach and grabbed the bottle of whiskey and took a swig before the bartender or Eric could stop me. I tossed the cash on the bar top and walked away from Eric and toward the exit. I just wanted one night to be normal again. I wanted one night to find a guy to take my mind off of everything.

Halfway to the door, large hands grabbed me and pulled me against a large body. I looked up into the face of an older African American man. He was attractive and scared the crap out of me at the same time. I didn't need my third eye to tell that he wasn't human. I tried to pull away from him and he ran his hand down my back to cup my ass. "Damn girl. I never knew white girls could have an ass like this."

Eric pulled me out of the man's arms and said, "She's off limits, Jeremiah."

Jeremiah smiled, his white teeth bright against his black skin. "Sure thing, boss. No harm done."

I pulled away from Eric. "I'm not yours! You have no right to tell others I'm off limits."

Jeremiah laughed loudly, shaking my ear drums. "Oh, she's a live one. Let me know how long it takes for her growl to change to a purr."

I glared at Jeremiah and walked through the rest of the people and out of the club. The cold night air stole my breath and chilled me in an instant. I looked around for a winter fairy, wondering if they were playing a prank on me, but my eye was still closed so everyone looked human. I tried looking out of the corner of my eye, but the alcohol was blurring my normal vision so even that trick was useless. Eric came out of the club and I started walking toward my house. "Ciara, wait."

I ignored him and kept walking down the sidewalk. I made it two blocks before someone stepped out of the alley and reached for me. What was going on tonight? Did I have a big sign over my head that said Seer?

I tried to kick him, but had drunk too much and ended up barely grazing him and falling. The man reached for me and then Eric hit him. I stood up and rubbed my shoulder which had taken the brunt of the fall. I heard growling next to me and stepped between Eric and the other man. "Back off tiger-boy. Go find some other meal." I didn't actually know if he was a tiger, but for some reason that was the vibe he was giving me.

The man glared at me, then ran down the alley, disappearing in seconds. I hated how fast they were. It was completely unfair. Eric turned me around and glared down at me. "I told you not to do something like that again."

I shook my head. "You have no idea what there really is out there. He could have ripped you apart before you blinked. I am not worth getting mauled."

Eric sighed and rubbed his eyes. "I can take care of myself, Ciara."

I glared at him. "So, can I!"

He stared at me in silence for a few seconds then sighed. "Alright. I'm sorry."

My eyes widened in shock. He just apologized?! I nodded at him then started walking down the sidewalk again. Eric matched my strides and I stopped again, "What are you doing?"

He smiled. "Walking you home."

I frowned. "I told you that I can't do this. You're my boss…" Tigerboy leapt at me from the alleyway, interrupting me and slammed me to the ground. My head hit the pavement and the world went black.

FOUR

I woke up with a warm washcloth being pressed to the side of my head. I tried to push it away, but warm hands held me down. "It's alright Ciara. It's just me."

I opened my eyes slowly and frowned. "Eric? What... where are we?"

He rinsed the washcloth in a bowl then pushed it on my head again. Pain sizzled in my head and I whimpered pathetically. "I'm sorry it hurts, but I have to clean it."

I swallowed and asked again, "Where are we?"

He pushed back a strand of hair that was on my face. "At your house."

"But you didn't know where I lived," I whispered.

He smiled. "Your address was programmed into the phones and a few of your neighbors were out so I asked them which house was yours."

I sighed and then hissed as he pushed harder on the wound on my head. "What happened?"

Eric's face hardened and his eyes glowed. "That boy

34

jumped on you and you hit your head on the sidewalk. I pulled him off of you and after a brief tumble he ran off."

I stared at him in shock. "He ran away? They don't run away."

Eric shrugged. "I called his bluff. Men really aren't that tough." He ran a hand along my throat where the scratch from the knife was. I pulled away from him and tried to stand, but the pain in my head forced me to my knees. Eric picked me up and put me back on the bed. "Stop it. I'm not going to hurt you."

I asked, "What are you?"

He frowned. "A man that is worried about his friend. Why do they keep calling you, Seer?"

I opened my mouth then closed it again. "I don't know."

Eric gave me a lopsided smile. "Uh-huh. Are you hungry?"

The thought of food made my stomach roll. I crawled off the bed and hurried as fast as I could to the bathroom, promptly losing my lunch and everything else that was in my stomach. Eric sat down behind me and pulled my hair back. He was holding my hair while I puked, if I wasn't so grossed out, I would think it was cute. I finished throwing everything up and wiped my mouth with toilet paper. "You don't have to do this," I whispered without looking at him.

Eric handed me a glass of water. "Drink this."

I sipped the water slowly and slumped against the toilet. "Maybe I had, had enough."

Eric laughed softly. "I believe so. Are you feeling better?"

I stood up and brushed my teeth quickly before answering him. "Yes."

He helped me back to my bed and started bandaging my head. "It's a small gash, but you need to keep it clean."

I looked up at his worried face. "Thank you."

He frowned. "For what?"

I rolled my eyes then groaned as nausea hit me. "For taking care of me. No one's ever…it's nice of you."

He pulled my tennis shoes and socks off. "Do you have anyone who can come help you?"

I started to shake my head then remembered the injury. "No, but I'll be fine."

Eric shook his head and started rubbing my feet. I sighed in pleasure and he said, "I'll stay with you. You have to be careful of head injuries, especially since you blacked out for ten minutes or so."

I tried to pull my foot away, but Eric just put it back in his lap and continued rubbing it. "Eric, you really don't have to…"

Eric sighed. "Stop it. I'm staying and there's nothing you can do about it." He traded feet and started working out all of the tension in the other one.

I closed my eyes and felt near unconscious when Eric smacked my foot making me open my eyes. "Stay awake, Ciara."

"You're putting me to sleep." I mumbled.

He set my foot down and smiled seductively at me. "I could think of a few ways to keep you up."

I swallowed as my heart rate picked up and my body heated up. "I told you that…"

Eric sighed. "I was just kidding, stop acting so serious. Would you like some tea?"

I nodded and Eric picked me up in his arms. "Wha…what are you doing?"

He smiled. "Taking you to the kitchen to get some tea."

I frowned. "I can walk."

He shook his head. "No, you can't."

I leaned my head against his shoulder hoping the dizziness

would go away and giving in to the desire. "Whatever." I knew it sounded half hearted, but I didn't care anymore. He was warm and being nice. The least I could do was enjoy it. He set me down on one of the barstools and started making tea for us. I watched him move around my kitchen and a tiny sparkle of delight settled in my stomach at the thought of him being here all night. He set my cup in front of me and then sat across the kitchen's island to face me. I asked, "So, how come all of those guys at the club knew you?"

"I own the club," He said nonchalantly between sips of tea.

I stared at him in shock. "You own it?" He nodded. "No wonder the bartender was waiting for your approval to give me a drink."

He frowned. "Yes, well apparently you don't listen to me as well as he does."

I smiled. "I'm your employee seven am to six pm, Monday through Friday. After that I'm my own woman."

He smiled. "I saw that."

I stared down at my tea and sighed. "You should probably leave though. It's not safe here."

"Oh, are you a danger to me?" He asked with amusement in his voice.

I rolled my eyes. "Obviously not."

"Are you in trouble?" He asked sincerely.

I looked up at his worried face. "It's nothing I can't handle, but I wouldn't want you to be caught in the middle if something did happen."

Eric reached out and set his hand on mine. "I can take care of myself and I'm not leaving tonight." I blushed and looked down. Eric whispered, "I know you're worried because I'm your boss, but right now I'm not your boss. I'm your friend."

I took a sip from the tea and he pulled his hand back. I

wanted to say something about him not even knowing me, but the truth was I wanted him here. I wanted him to stay with me. The tea warmed me and I started feeling tired. Eric took the tea and picked me up in his arms. "I think we need a change of scenery and a way to keep you awake for a few more hours."

I groaned. "Hours? I don't think I can stay up a few more hours."

He carried me in to the living room and set me down on the couch. He started sorting through my CD's and smiled. "I guess you don't like quiet?"

I shrugged. "I've learned that some of the nastier things don't like loud noises."

He looked at me in shock. "Nastier things? Like what?"

Shit. "Uh, like bears." I said quickly.

He frowned. "Bears? There aren't any bears in this area."

I smiled. "Or maybe I've just scared them all away with my music."

He laughed and started going through my movies. "Ah, here is one of my favorite movies. We'll watch this, then you should be able to go to sleep."

I tried to see what he was putting in, but he hid it and turned on the television. I pulled the afghan off the back of the couch and wrapped myself in it. Eric pressed play and I stared at him in shock. "This is one of your favorites?"

He smiled. "Does that surprise you?"

"Of course it does. Moulin Rouge is a total chick flick." I said with a smile on my face.

Eric frowned. "Real men aren't afraid to cry at sentimental movies."

I laughed softly. "Oh, you are definitely not an average lawyer."

He sat down next to me. "Is that a bad thing?"

"No, not at all. Actually, it's refreshing."

He hit play and moved an inch closer to me. I could feel the heat radiating off of him and my body relaxed. I had never met a man that was so easy to be around. Of course, that might have been due to the fact that a lot of the men in this town weren't human. I closed my eyes and focused on my third eye. I imagined seeing people's true faces and pleaded with my mind to open. I opened my eyes and looked at Eric, but still only saw a man. He asked, "Do you have a headache?"

I sighed. "No, it's nothing." I wrapped the blanket around me tighter and settled in to watch the movie. It was no use straining myself now, although the thought of graveling to Akio wasn't appealing either. I watched as the actors danced and sung and told their tragic story and my eyelids started growing heavy. My eyes closed a few times and I found myself lying with my head on Eric's shoulder. He watched the movie intently and I decided that if he cared, he would push me off of him and besides I was way too comfortable to care. The movie ended and Eric picked me up in his arms. He turned off the lights and television then checked the locks. I didn't weigh much, but I knew I had to be getting heavy. "Eric, I can walk."

He shushed me and carried me up the stairs. He didn't groan or grunt as he carried me to my room and laid me down on my bed like I was as light as a child. He turned off the light and sat down in the leather recliner at the other end of my room. I frowned. "When did you bring the chair up to my room?"

He laughed softly. "While you were sleeping during the movie."

"I'm sorry. I've been very impolite tonight."

Eric walked over and smoothed my hair away from my

face and pulled my blankets up. "Go to sleep, Ciara. I'll be here when you wake up and nothing will happen to you while I'm here."

I scoffed softly. "I'm not worried about me."

He shook his head. "I told you I can take care of myself. Now go to sleep."

I tried to protest, but sleep yanked away my free will and everything went black and became peaceful.

The morning sun pressed against my skull and I groaned. "Five more minutes."

A quite male voice answered, "I don't think the sun will listen to you. It has a mind of its own."

I bolted upright in bed and moaned in pain as dizziness forced me on to my back. Eric rushed over to my bed. "I didn't mean to frighten you."

I put my arm over my face to block the sunlight. "I forgot that you were here."

He sighed sadly. "Am I so easily forgotten?"

I moved my arm up and saw his teasing smile. "It's too early to banter."

He scoffed. "It's ten o'clock. I believe bantering starts at eight."

"Ten? Crap. I haven't slept this late in years."

I tried to sit up, but Eric pushed me back down. "Just stay in bed. You don't have anything you have to do."

I sat up slowly. "I have to do my workout. Hangovers are no reason to miss workouts." I reached up and touched my wound. "And neither are physical wounds." I slowly swung my legs out of the covers and shivered. "Did you turn on the air conditioner?"

He smiled. "Sorry, I was hot and you seemed plenty warm under the blankets. I'll go turn it off."

I shook my head. "No, it's alright. It'll be another distraction for me to deal with." I hurried across the room and to the bathroom and quickly brushed my teeth, used the restroom and combed my hair. I put my hair up in a ponytail and stared at my sallow reflection. Note to self, do not drink that much ever again. I walked out of the bathroom, but Eric wasn't there. I walked slowly down the stairs and into the kitchen where I could hear pots and pans being moved around. Eric was breaking eggs in to a bowl and had bacon starting on the stove. "Okay, now I feel awful. Let me make breakfast at least. You babysat me all night and it's only fair that I make the breakfast."

Eric ignored me and continued to break eggs into the bowel. I grabbed his hand as he started to crack another one and his lip twitched. He shook his head and smiled. "Alright, since you insist, but I want it noted that I have no objection to making breakfast."

I smiled. "Your comment has been noted for the record. Now sit down and let me make breakfast."

He set the egg down and reached towards my head then stopped. "May I check your wound?"

My heart rate sped up and I nodded. He stood an inch away from me and lifted the bandage on the side of my head. He nodded and smoothed it back down. "It's better. You're healing very fast actually." He let his hand slide down my head to my face and stroked his thumb across my cheek. "Are you feeling alright?"

My body moved forward against my will and pressed against his. "Yes."

He bent down slowly and kissed my cheek softly. "Good."

My cheeks flared as blood rushed to them. I turned away from him and flipped the bacon. He sat down in one of the barstools on the other side of the island pretending not to notice my blush. I finished making breakfast and made our plates, sliding his to him. I sat across from him so my body wouldn't try to touch him against my will again and we ate in silence. When we finished, he insisted on helping me do the dishes and we worked side by side at the sink. I found myself craving the casual touches he gave me and decided to let him finish the dishes alone. I hid in the bathroom for a few minutes as I tried to calm my hormones. It wasn't working. I walked out of the bathroom and found him watching television. I started to go towards him when someone knocked on my front door. I looked at it in shock. No one ever came here. I started to go toward it when Eric stopped me. "Let me get it."

I frowned. "Eric, it's my house."

"What if it's…"

I waved my hand and hurried to the door. Two muscular men who looked like they'd been using a little too much juice stood on the doorstep. I opened the door a crack and asked, "Can I help you?"

The men looked nervous and started fidgeting with their hands. Finally, one of them spoke, "Is Eric here?"

"Uh, yeah. Hold on." I shut the door and locked it before walking to the living room. "It's for you."

He groaned. "Never a peaceful moment." He walked to the front door and spoke so quietly to the men that I couldn't hear what they were talking about. Eric came back a minute later looking very angry. "I have to go. Something happened at the club last night that I need to take care of today."

"Okay. Thanks for everything last night."

He jiggled his car keys looking nervous then rushed forward and kissed me on the lips. Fire exploded through me and my hands found their way behind his neck and into his hair. He wrapped his arms around my waist and pulled me against him. The image of us working together flashed across my closed eyelids and I yanked back from him gasping for air. He smiled and shook his head. "You are an interesting person. Would it be alright if I came back to check on you tonight?"

I nodded and he left the house. Shit. Shit. Shit. I was breaking every rule in the book now. Getting involved with my boss was murder! I'd have to quit. I'd have to call him and quit before he came over tonight. Why couldn't my hormones stop acting so crazy?

I needed a distraction so I turned on Slipknot and started my exercises. I needed to clear my head and go to Akio soon because as much as I hated to admit it my third eye had to open again. I took a cleansing breath and started my routine, but no matter how hard I tried to clear my vision I could only see Eric's face and feel his lips on mine. Two hours of trying later and I gave up. I had it bad and I had only known him for a few weeks.

I put in another movie and tried to entertain myself, but all I could think about was Eric. I finally decided to go for a run and locked up my house. My body healed a little faster than a normal human's so my head wouldn't hurt as I ran. I ran into the forest and down the nature trail, which was my favorite place to go to get away from people. The birds chirped loudly as I ran past and the cool air cleared my thoughts. I jogged the trail twice then went back to the house. I showered and changed and sat at the television and waited for Eric. The day turned to night and he didn't come or stop by. I sighed. Who was I kidding? An attractive man like him wouldn't be seriously interested in me. I would be just another notch on his belt. I stormed up to my room and read my book, becoming lost in the story and forgetting my life. It was the best therapy I had. Sunday was worse than Saturday and Eric never called. Was he hurt? Maybe he had gotten attacked by one of the guys he protected me from? I picked up my phone and dialed his phone number. I stared at his number on my phone and cleared it. I wouldn't be the needy girl. I couldn't be the needy girl. We hadn't even had a date or anything. I flopped down on my bed to go to sleep when my phone rang. I answered quickly, "Hello?"

Eric laughed softly. "Did I wake you?"

"Uh, yeah. What's up?" I rolled my eyes. Great conversation starter.

"I just wanted to apologize for not contacting you yesterday. It was the full moon and as you know this town gets a little crazy then. Well I had a lot to deal with at the club."

I interrupted him. "It's alright. You don't have to explain yourself to me."

He exhaled then asked, "Will you go to dinner with me tomorrow?"

I stared at the phone in shock. "Eric...I..."

He interrupted me. "I know you are worried about me being your boss, but I like you..."

I shook my head then realized he couldn't see me. "I'm sorry Eric, but I can't. I just can't risk ruining my career."

He sighed and spoke very softly, "Alright. I understand. I'll see you tomorrow."

"Eric it's nothing against you..."

He interrupted me again. "It's alright, Ciara. I'll see you tomorrow."

Great. I hadn't thought about the possibility of losing my job for turning down my boss. "Okay, remember that we have a meet and confer at ten tomorrow."

Eric scoffed. "I know. Have a good night Ciara."

"You too."

I hung up the phone and groaned. Dammit all to heck. Now he was pissed. Lawyers always got quiet when they were pissed. He was probably going to go to the Chief and tell him to fire me. Shit. I shoved a pillow over my mouth and screamed into it. Why couldn't I have an easy, normal life? Why me? I screamed again in to the pillow then closed my eyes to go back to sleep.

I got to work at seven o'clock, before Eric arrived and pulled all of the files he needed for the day and arranged them on his desk in appointment order. Then I hurried to the kitchen and made him a cup of his favorite tea, adding one scoop of sugar and then grabbed two donuts and put them on a plate. I hurried back to his office and had them on his desk just as he walked in his door.

He smiled. "You're here early."

I smiled. "Just being efficient." I hurried out of his office and to my desk. I stared at the single red rose sitting on my keyboard. I could hear Eric sipping his tea and flipping through one of the files. I set the rose down next to my computer and started working trying not to think about what the rose meant. My alarm went off to notify him of his conference so I walked in to his office and cleared my throat. "Your conference is in ten minutes."

Eric nodded. "Thanks." I turned to walk away and Eric's voice stopped me. "Ciara." I turned around and he smiled. "You look great today."

I blushed and looked down at the dress. "Thank you." I hurried to my desk and put my headphones on to listen to his dictation. He waved as he walked out of my office and I sighed. Shit. This was going to be harder than I thought. I kept my head buried in the computer the rest of the day and hurried home right at six. My night was uneventful as usual and I got to work early again so that his tea, donuts and files were on his desk when he arrived. I used the restroom an hour later and when I came back a red rose was waiting for me on my keyboard again. I smelled the flower and put it on my desk next to the other one. This I could get used to.

At lunch Eric asked me to join him to discuss a case so I agreed. He took me to my favorite Italian restaurant and except for the occasional look by me, it was completely professional. As we walked into his office, I realized just how badly I wanted him. I stopped at his doorway as he continued to his chair and took a deep reassuring breath. "I'm quitting."

Eric stopped in mid-sit and looked at me. "You're what?"

"Quitting. I'm sorry, but you'll find a new secretary."

Eric shook his head and stood up. "I don't want a new secretary. Is it something I've done? Do you want more money? What is it?"

I sighed. "It's...I just can't work..."

He walked forward and closed the door to his office, pulling me inside and pulled down the blinds. "Whatever it is just tell me."

I blushed and the words tumbled out before I could stop them. "It's too difficult to work with you when all I can think about is how much I want to touch you."

I gasped and put a hand over my mouth. Eric smiled and picked my hand up in his. "Then touch me." He pulled my hand up to his cheek and smiled wider. "We can make this work. I'll do whatever you want."

I wanted to step back and stop touching him, but I couldn't. "I...secretaries and bosses can't date."

He shrugged. "Then we don't have to date." He bent down

and kissed my lips softly. "We can do whatever you want as long as you stay with me."

I swallowed the desire to jump on him and whispered, "I'll stay, but no dating."

He smiled. "Good." He kissed my lips and stroked my cheek. "Don't scare me like that again. You're too valuable to lose."

I swallowed and stepped back from him. "Okay." I walked out of his room and sat down at my desk. Well that had worked. Damn I had it so bad. How can one man have this much of an effect on me?

I stared at the roses on my desk and the sticky note on the corner of my monitor and sighed. There had to be some way to work this out. A tall dark-haired woman walked to my door and smiled. "I'm here to speak to Eric." I looked at her naturally tan skin and black hair and long slim body and was instantly jealous.

I smiled and asked, "I don't believe you have an appointment. May I ask what this is regarding?"

She laughed and I despised her more for her bubbly girly laugh. "Oh, it's personal sweetheart. Just tell him that Sugar is here."

I smiled at her and walked in to his office partially shutting the door. "Eric, Sugar is here to see you. She says it's personal."

Eric's eyes widened a fraction and then he smiled. "Let her in."

I nodded and walked back to my office where Sugar was smelling one of my roses. "Mr. Wolfe will see you now."

She set my rose down and winked. "Thanks sweetheart." I watched as she sashayed in to his office like a Latino seductress Barbie and felt my anger building. She shut the door and

I snapped a pencil in half that I had picked up. How stupid could I be? Of course an attractive man like Eric would have girls like her. I tossed the pencil on my desk, put my headphones on and started typing a pleading that I had started earlier in the day. I was printing the pleading when Eric and Sugar walked out of his office. Sugar kissed Eric on the cheek and smiled flirtatiously. "Let me know if you need anything else."

Eric nodded, "Always a pleasure Sugar. Tell that alpha of yours I said hi."

Alpha? She winked at me as she walked out. "Wish I had your job sweetheart."

I glared at her back as she laughed and walked out of the office. I grabbed the pleading from the printer and turned to hand it to Eric, but he was playing with the broken pencil on my desk. "Bad day?"

I handed him the papers, "I need your signature on this." He searched my face, but I kept it carefully blank. He took a pen out of his jacket pocket and signed his name in that perfect elegant script he had.

He handed me the papers and frowned, "Ciara…"

I interrupted him. "You should straighten your tie. You have a meeting in five minutes and I'm sure you don't want rumors spread around the office." Especially if they concern me. The Latino seductress he would probably be proud to boast about.

Eric frowned harder. "Ciara it's not what you think…"

I shrugged and sat down at my desk, putting my headphones on. "I don't get paid to think Mr. Wolfe." I pressed the foot pedal to start the tape and started typing. I could feel Eric still standing behind me, but focused on my work. A full minute passed before he walked into his office and grabbed his briefcase before walking out of my office to go to the conference room for his next meeting. I stopped typing and sighed. Way to act like the jealous girlfriend. Dammit. I walked to the copy machine and started making my copies, ignoring the stares of the other secretaries. I gathered up my copies and walked to the mail area. One of the secretaries stood up and smiled at me. "Bad day?"

I sighed. "Yes."

She shrugged. "Every attorney has flaws. You just have to learn to ignore them or else they eat you up inside until you can't work for that attorney. It's like a marriage in a way. If you and your attorney aren't on the same level you won't make good partners, but if you are then you make the perfect team and that's really how attorneys win cases. It's also why secretaries and attorneys end up marrying a lot."

I looked up at her. "What? I've never heard of that."

She laughed. "Oh, it happens quite often. Most of the time they just keep it a secret so you just think the boss shouldn't be messing with his secretary 'til you find out one day she's also his wife. Then you decide that they must have one hell of a sex life since you know they get it on in his office. Man, how hot would that be?"

I stared at her in shock. "So, you're saying that a lot of the attorneys here that we think are just messing with their secretaries are really married to them?"

The secretary nodded. "Every one of the attorneys here on the first floor, excepting Mr. Wolfe, is married to their secretaries."

I finished closing the envelopes I had been working on and set them in the outgoing basket. "Wow."

The secretary smiled. "I'm Rose by the way."

I extended my hand to her. "Ciara."

She shook my hand and winked. "Now try and work it out with Mr. Wolfe. He seems like a nice guy. And single is always good when they look like him."

She giggled and sat back down at her desk and started typing. I walked slowly back to my desk replaying what she had said to me. This whole time I had thought that the secretaries were breaking the cardinal rule of law offices when really, they were just having fun with their husbands. I sat down at my desk and started a new pleading. I was so focused that I didn't notice Eric until he touched my shoulder. I jumped up and unplugged my headphones. Eric smiled. "Sorry, I didn't mean to scare you."

I swallowed the lump in my throat and shook my head. "'S alright." I took off my headphones and set them on the desk. "Did you need something?"

He frowned. "I wanted to explain…"

I shook my head. "You don't need to explain anything. What you do in your office is your business, not mine."

Eric sighed. "But nothing happened, Ciara." I walked into his office and grabbed a file from one of his shelves that I needed for the pleading. I turned around and Eric grabbed my arms with his hands. "Ciara, listen to me. Sugar is a friend and that's all. Nothing happened."

I frowned. "I don't know why you're telling me this. I'm just your secretary."

He groaned and shut his door and turned the blinds so no one could see inside. "You are *not* just my secretary." He took the file from my hands and tossed it on a nearby chair. "I care about you and I want you to know the truth."

I swallowed and backed up, but ran in to the shelf. "Mr. Wolfe, you…"

He growled. "Stop calling me that! If I wanted you to call

me that I wouldn't do this." He reached forward and pulled me against him kissing my lips bruising hard. My body melted into his touch, but I forced my hands to stay by my sides. He pulled back and searched my face. "Tell me that you don't have feelings for me? Tell me that you don't want to kiss me as much as I do you?"

I opened my mouth to say it, but it wasn't true and Rose's words came back to me. I looked down. "I do have feelings for you, but..."

He tilted my chin up and shook his head. "There is no but. Let me take you out tonight, anywhere you like."

I frowned. "I thought we agreed on not dating."

He smiled. "Then it won't be a date. Just two friends going out together to have some fun."

I smiled. "Bowling."

He raised an eyebrow in surprise, "Bowling? You want me to take you bowling? I offer to take you anywhere and you choose bowling?"

I shrugged and tried to pull away from him. "If you don't want to go..."

He pulled me back into his arms and shook his head. "Bowling is fine. Can we go to dinner first?"

I stared in to his golden-brown eyes and gave in. "Sure."

He rubbed his cheek against mine and nipped my earlobe. "Mexican?"

I shivered against him and whispered, "Sure."

He rubbed his cheek along the other side of my face and I jumped backwards. "Why are you doing that?" It was a classic wereanimal sign of possession. Rubbing his face against mine like that would leave his scent on me for the rest of the day.

He frowned. "I just like touching you. Why are you so

jumpy? You act like you think I'm going to attack you or something."

"Sorry, it's just…never mind." I said as I ran a hand through my hair. Was I crazy to keep comparing him to preternaturals?

He kissed my lips softly. "I only talked with Sugar. She was passing on a message from her boss to me. That's all." He kissed my lips again. "I am not seeing anyone else and am not being intimate with anyone. I don't expect you to give me the same offer, but I wanted to let you know."

I frowned. "You mean you're being exclusive with me?"

He nodded and ran his hand up and down my back slowly. "Yes."

"You hardly know me," I whispered.

"I know enough and I know I'll learn more the more time we spend together," he whispered back.

I swallowed. "You want me to be exclusive with you?"

He shrugged. "It's your decision, but I would like it."

It wasn't a tough decision. I smiled. "I'm not seeing anyone."

He smiled. "Except me?"

I rolled my eyes. "Right."

He exhaled a loud breath. "Good." He fiercely kissed me then whispered, "I don't like the idea of having to share you."

I smiled. "Me either."

He rolled his eyes. "I noticed the pencil."

I blushed. "Anger is a natural emotion."

He licked my top lip. "And very attractive on you."

I knew if I didn't move away from him soon that I would find out just how attractive he thought it was. It took all of my willpower to pull away from him, "We can go to dinner straight from work if you want."

He smiled. "Sure. I have a change of clothes here."

I grabbed the file and walked back to my desk. What the hell had I started? I didn't even know what he wanted in life. I took my anger out on the keyboard and didn't stop the rest of the day. At six Eric made me stop so I could change. I shut down my computer and organized my desk and grabbed my backpack with my change of clothes. I changed quickly and re-brushed my hair and reapplied makeup. When I walked out of the bathroom Eric was leaning against the opposite wall of the hallway looking as scrumptious as ever. He looked even sexier in jeans and a t-shirt than I could have imagined. And he was definitely muscular. He smiled. "Are you ready?"

I nodded and followed him out of the back door to the employee parking lot. He held the car door open for me and I climbed in. He set a black velvet bag in my lap and started the car. I stared at the bag in shock. "What's this?"

He smiled as he got in. "A gift."

I frowned. "But you didn't know I was going out with you tonight."

He shrugged. "I was hoping you would some time this week so I kept it in here. Go on, open it."

I untied the black velvet bag and tipped it upside down. A small white gold ring with a Claddagh symbol on it fell in to my hand. My eyes widened in shock and I stared at Eric. He held up his hand stopping me from talking. "It's not an engagement ring. It's a Claddagh. If you are taken you wear the ring with the heart pointing towards you. If you're single you wear the ring with the heart pointing away from you. You don't have to wear it if you don't like."

I stared at the ring in shock remembering a scene from my favorite television show where the man had given the ring to his girlfriend. I was well aware of its meaning. I slipped the ring onto my left hand with the heart pointing towards me. "It's beautiful." He drove us to the most expensive Mexican restaurant in town and let a valet park the car. I was pleased as we walked to our table that he hadn't tried to hold my hand, but also a little disappointed. I knew I couldn't have it both ways, but my feelings didn't.

We sat in a booth in the back of the restaurant, but a waitress quickly came over, drooling over Eric. "Are you ready to order or would you like to order drinks first?"

Eric smiled. "Ciara?"

I smiled back at him, loving the envious look the waitress was giving me. "I'll have the steak fajitas and a mudslide."

Eric raised an eyebrow. "I'll have fajitas as well, but make mine chicken and a glass of water."

The waitress smiled at him. "Of course. I'll be right back with your drinks."

I shook my head. "That's the first time I haven't been carded."

He laughed. "Trust me when you get older you want them to card you. So, a mudslide, huh?"

I nodded. "What isn't there to like about a drink that tastes like a milkshake but is alcoholic? It's perfect."

The waitress brought our drinks and a basket of chips and salsa. I ate two chips and sipped my drink. Eric smiled at me. "So, have you always wanted to be a legal secretary?"

I laughed. "No. I didn't really *want* to be anything growing up." Except normal. "But the job was the easiest for me in my circumstance."

Eric frowned. "You keep talking about your circumstances, but not what they are."

"It's better if you don't know."

"Ciara, I'm not as fragile as you think."

I chewed up another chip and asked, "Did you always want to be an attorney?"

He frowned at me for changing the subject. "No, I was in the military for awhile, and then decided I needed a change of pace."

I looked down at my drink. "So, what do you want now?"

He was quiet for a moment and then spoke quietly, "I want someone to spend the rest of my life with. Just one person who will stay with me through the tough spots and love me for who I am. Right now, I can't imagine having kids, but things change and I wouldn't presume to be set on having kids or not without consulting my significant other. What about you?"

"Are you opposed to getting married?" I asked.

Eric smiled. "Not at all. Of course there are some women nowadays who feel marriage is just a way for men to tie them down. So, I'm open."

The waitress came back with our food, giving me a chance to be silent. The food was delicious and filled me up. Eric paid and then we drove to the bowling alley. After obtaining our rental shoes and picking out our balls we set up the game in lane sixteen, the lane I tried to reserve each time. Eric stood on the edge of the lane holding the ball in his hands. He took two steps forward then released the ball. I watched as every single pin fell. Eric smiled. "Strike."

I rolled my eyes. "Of course you're good at bowling. Is there anything you aren't good at?"

Eric tapped his chin thoughtfully as I waited for the pins to be reset. "Nothing comes to mind."

I rolled my eyes again. "You are no Wesley."

Eric smiled. "No, I believe I am much more handsome and better educated than Wesley."

I took a step toward the lane. "Wesley couldn't be educated except for what he taught himself because he was just a farm boy. Buttercup still loved him though." I threw the ball down the lane and sighed as it took out only four pins. It was actually fun to banter about the movie Princess Bride.

I walked back and waited for the ball to come up. Eric sighed. "If only women were so easy today."

I scoffed. "Some still are. As long as you're human, straight and kind, you pass my tests."

Eric's face fell slightly. "You are very persistent about human. Are you aware of aliens living here that I'm not?"

I picked my ball up as it was pushed up out of the floor on the conveyer. "You wouldn't believe me if I told you." I threw the ball and smiled happily as the rest of the pins fell. "Spare."

Eric stood up and stopped in front of me blocking my path. "Ciara, I wish you would talk to me."

I looked up in to his sincere face and tried to open my third eye. Nothing happened. "What if I told you that the fairy tales we had been told when we were children, are true? That fairy tales were meant as warnings to humans? What if I told you that fifty percent of the people in this town aren't human?"

Eric smiled. "I'd believe you. I'd also be curious as to how you would know."

I shrugged. "Some call it a gift. I think it's a curse. Either way it draws their attention and that is never a good thing."

Eric frowned. "So, you can see them when humans can't?"

"Even when other beings can't," I whispered.

Eric took my hand in his. "And that makes you a target? Which is why you said I shouldn't be around you?"

"Especially why you shouldn't be around me. If they were to hurt you I…"

Eric kissed my lips softly. "I can protect myself."

"How can you protect yourself from something you can't See? They look completely human to others, but their real faces are often horrible."

Eric frowned. "Are they all bad?"

"Oh, no. Everyone on our first floor is a preternatural and none of them have tried to harm me, yet."

Eric's eyes opened in surprise. "That's why Mr. Wallace attacked you. He knew you could see what he really looked like."

I nodded. "Yep. He thought I was sent there to find him and take him back to the wereanimals."

Eric frowned. "Why would the wereanimals want him?"

"He was probably a slave or something. Preternaturals aren't humanitarians like the humans. Most are very barbaric and animalistic, but that's to be expected from some who are animals half of the time."

Eric asked, "And what do you think about wereanimals?"

I shrugged. "I haven't really talked to many of them, but the ones that I have are very single minded."

Eric raised an eyebrow in question. "How so?"

I took his ball and tossed it in to the gutter. "Sex is all they think about."

Eric frowned. "That was my shot."

I shrugged. "You took too long."

Eric waited for his ball to come and then tossed it down the center of the lane getting a strike. Bastard. "So, what happens if they find out you can see them?"

I looked down at the ground. "I try not to think about that. Let's just say that there aren't very many positive possibilities."

Eric reached out to console me, but I pulled away and

grabbed my ball. I tossed it down the lane and grimaced as it swung in to the gutter. Eric laughed quietly and I spun around glaring at him. "Not all of us can be perfect you know."

Eric's laughter faded and his smile disappeared. "I'm far from perfect."

"Right. Because there's nothing you aren't good at?"

He shook his head. "That was bantering. If I wasn't so self-ish, I would be pushing you away and telling you to run, but I can't push you away."

He started walking toward me and I couldn't move. The openness of his words and the fragile look on his face as if he expected me to turn him away forced me to stay and listen. He stopped in front of me. "I've never felt this way about a woman before. I know you're worried for my safety, but I assure you that I can take care of myself. It is much more damaging for me to be away from you. I've tried to ignore it, but you are too much. Your scent, your face, your body. It all draws me in and I can't ignore my cravings."

I swallowed. "Eric, I..."

He put his finger over my lips. "I don't want you to say anything. I just want you to know how I feel." His finger was replaced by his lips as he kissed me.

I kissed him back then whispered, "Let's go to my house."

He smiled and nodded. "Okay." We hurried out of the bowling alley and into his car. He drove fifty the entire way and slammed on his brakes in front of my house. I grabbed his hand and led him to my front door then stopped. The door wasn't closed and the handle was missing. Eric looked at the door handle and pulled me behind him. "Wait here."

I shook my head and grabbed his arm. "No. Let's just go."

Eric frowned. "Ciara, just stay here." He pulled out of my grip and entered the house, opening the door silently. I danced from foot to foot as I waited for the scream, I knew I would hear. Two minutes passed before the first growl came, but it wasn't inside. I turned to the right slowly and tensed. Two set of glowing eyes looked at me from the forest. I started to take a step toward the front door when another growl sounded and a large rat hissed at me.

"Oh, come on. Rodents of unusual size? Why me?" I asked angrily. I backed up slowly and then saw Eric run out of the front door. He grabbed the wererat around the throat and tossed it out of the house toward the trees and his friends. Eric picked me up and started running. "Eric, you can't outrun them!" I yelled.

He smiled. "I can try." He picked up a little speed, but when I looked behind us the rats were right on our tails.

"What did they use in the fire swamp?" I asked out loud.

Eric sighed. "Ciara, that's just a book turned into a movie."

"Shows what you know. Stories stem from truth. Now find some fire and a sword. Oh, the dojo! Straight up the street five blocks and on the left."

Eric sighed in disbelief. "Ciara…"

I smiled. "Oh, come on, Wesley."

He smiled at me. "As you wish." He picked up even more speed just keeping the rats out of reach of us. They were hideous monstrosities. Rats the size of Saint Bernard's with beady red eyes.

Eric ran up the dojo's steps and I yelled, "Akio! Rats!"

Akio flung open the door to the dojo and Eric darted inside. Akio snapped, "Turn away."

Eric set me down and I turned him to face the back wall. "He doesn't like an audience when he's working."

Eric raised a questioning eyebrow, but stayed facing the wall with me. Bones popped and snapped and the air heated up around us as Akio changed. The rats' nails clicked on the steps as they charged up and then they hissed in fear. A roar of rage sounded and then the oxygen was sucked from the air and fire plumed behind us. Eric started to turn his head, but I stepped between him and the wall and pulled his face down to mine. He kissed me back like he was taking his first breath of air. I wrapped my hands in his thick hair and pressed my body to his. He pressed me against the wall and the kiss intensified as he searched every part of my mouth as if to memorize me. His hands ran up and down my body and settled on my lower back and neck. The sound of dying rats and burning hair was barely noticeable in the moment of our kiss. Nothing mattered, but Eric.

Akio cleared his throat and I released Eric's hair. He stepped back from me with still closed eyes. "I'm sorry. That was out of line," Eric said quietly.

I laughed softly. "I should be the one apologizing. You just saved me and I forced the kiss."

Akio cleared his throat again. "Explain."

Eric looked down at his watch. "I hate to do this, but I have to go. Are you going to be alright?"

I nodded. "I'll stay here at the dojo with Akio. They won't try to get me here."

Akio tried to get a better look at Eric, but Eric kissed my lips and jogged out of the dojo. "I'll call you tomorrow."

I watched as his plump butt flexed and relaxed with each step. Akio scoffed. "Hormones."

I smiled. "Sorry. Can I have some tea before I explain?"

Akio nodded then looked at the doorway. "We should dispose of the bodies first."

I groaned. "I hate cleanup duty."

FIVE

After we had disposed of the bodies we sat down to tea in the middle of the dojo. "Eric and I were walking up to the house and I noticed the door was broken in. Eric went inside and then I noticed the rats in the forest and then a rat came out of the front door. Eric grabbed it around the throat and tossed it to the side dazing it and then he picked me up and started running. I had him come here because it was the only place I could think to run to. If those rats had hurt him, I wouldn't have been able to forgive myself."

Akio frowned, "Your eye is still closed I take it?"

I nodded. "Yes, but I don't need it open to see the wererats when they're in rat form."

Akio shook his head. "No, but the man..."

My cell phone rang and I interrupted Akio to answer it. "Hello?"

Eric sighed. "You're alright. Ciara, I need you to come to the club."

"But what if there are more rats?"

Eric spoke gruffly to someone near him. "I've sent someone to pick you up. Jeremiah will be there in a minute."

I frowned. "Okay, but what do you need me at the club for?"

Eric was silent for a moment then whispered, "I would feel better if I knew for sure that you were safe. I don't doubt that your sensei can hold his own, but it would just make me feel better. Please."

I don't know if it was the way he said please or the worry in his voice, but I agreed. "Alright."

Eric sighed in relief. "Thank you. Jeremiah should be there now." Two honks from a car sounded, confirming Jeremiah's arrival.

I laughed. "Alright I'm on my way." I hung up the phone and turned to Akio. "I'm going to go meet Eric. I'll be back tomorrow."

Akio frowned. "This man he is not what he seems."

I rolled my eyes. "No one is these days. I'll work on my eye too. Thank you for your protection, Master." I bowed to him and walked to the dojo door.

Akio spoke softly, "Be careful who you align yourself with, Ciara. There are many dangerous things I have not shown you."

I bowed to Akio again then walked out of the dojo and in to the open door that Jeremiah was holding. He smiled. "Evening."

I smiled back. "Hello Jeremiah."

He drove slowly to the club and opened my door for me when we arrived. Some of the patrons standing outside to smoke watched me with wary eyes, but none made any move towards me. It probably had to do with the mountain walking beside me. Jeremiah made a path for me through the club and to a roped off area where Eric and two other men were sitting. The two men glanced at me, and then left the area. Eric held out his hand, but I ignored it and sat down in the chair across from him. Eric smiled. "How is your master doing?"

I sighed. "Eric about what you saw. I know it must be hard to…"

Eric smiled. "I know about the preternaturals, Ciara. I don't think you can live in Luna Villa long without seeing them."

I stared at him in shock. "So, you know about the wererats?"

Eric nodded and gestured toward Jeremiah. "Werebear."

I giggled. "Werebear? Okay, it makes sense but you have to admit that it sounds funny."

Eric laughed softly. "True, but I wouldn't say that to his face. Did the rats hurt you at all?"

I shook my head. "No, they didn't get close enough, thanks to you."

Eric reached across the table and held his hand palm up. I stared at it for a moment and then placed my hand in his. Eric's shoulders relaxed. "Thank you."

I frowned. "For what?"

He squeezed my hand. "For not refusing a public sign of affection."

"Eric about that. I don't know…"

Eric shook his head. "Don't. Please just let me enjoy this night at least."

"Eric."

Eric smiled and moved to sit beside me. "So, what exactly were you planning when we got to your house?"

I blushed and stood up. "I need something to drink."

Eric grabbed my arm. "Let Jeremiah get it for you. I'd rather you didn't wander through the crowd."

"I'm not helpless." I said impatiently.

Eric raised his eyebrow. "Do you have some powers I'm not aware of?" I met his gaze, but knew I wouldn't win. How can you argue with a lawyer? Eric smiled and motioned Jeremiah over. Eric whispered in to Jeremiah's ear and Jeremiah left laughing loudly.

I folded my arms across my chest and glared at Eric. "So, what now?"

Eric shrugged then leaned back in his seat, reclining casually, but somehow looking as though he were posing for a photo shoot. "Whatever you want."

Jeremiah walked back through the crowd and set a glass down in front of me with whipped cream on the top. "One mudslide for the pretty Seer."

I frowned at him, but took a drink of the mudslide. It was amazing! "I don't understand how you can know that I'm a Seer. It's not the same thing as me seeing you. I don't have a difference face."

Two men started fighting over a woman and Jeremiah sighed. "Duty calls." He walked through the crowd and to the fighting men.

Eric cleared his throat. "Would you like to see a movie? Or maybe get some dessert?"

I shrugged. "I could go for some ice cream."

He smiled and stood up holding his hand out for mine. I stared at his hand and he sighed. "At least let me lead you through the dance floor."

I wanted to decline, but it was hard to get through the drunk dancers without getting a few elbows or stepped on toes without a man making way for you. I set my half empty glass down and took his hand. He walked down in to the throng of people towards the front door. We took a step outside and someone grabbed my arm pulling me backwards. I turned to see an angry male fairy, without any glamour on, glaring at me. "Why are you here Seer? Who sent you?"

I stared at him in shock. "I don't know what you're talking about. No one sent me."

The fairy glared at me and his skin began glowing. Glowing fairy equals major fight. "Was it the vampires?"

Eric pulled me backwards and stood toe to toe with the fairy. "Do not touch her ever again."

The fairy frowned at him. "Why are you interfering, Wolfe?"

Eric's lip twitched in a snarl. "I don't like the way you're handling my partner. It would be wise if you refrained from coming here again. I'm sure you're aware of my close relationship with Warrior?"

The fairy's skin stopped glowing and he dropped my arm. "You better keep your Seer on a leash. If she rats on any of us, I'll come looking for you."

Eric turned to Jeremiah who had randomly appeared. "Escort him out and be sure he does not return, ever."

Jeremiah smiled and even with my eye closed I could picture a bear snarling. "My pleasure."

Eric led me from the club and down the street. It felt nice to be holding hands with him and I decided to let myself enjoy it. We walked through the downtown streets and stopped at the local ice cream shop. Eric found us an empty seat and a waiter walked over smiling cheerfully. "Hey there. folks. What can I get you?"

Eric tapped his chin for a moment and I found myself

locked on his finger. "I'll have a sundae with three scoops of vanilla, no nuts."

The waiter turned to me and I smiled. "I'll have a waffle bowl with one scoop chocolate and two scoops of strawberry. Oh, and can you put a cherry on top? Thanks." The waiter walked away and Eric sat smiling at me. "What?" I asked.

He shrugged. "Just watching your eyes light up as you ordered the ice cream."

"I like ice cream," I said defensively.

Eric reached under the table and rested his hand on my knee. "I like you."

I sighed. "You're persistent."

Eric rubbed his thumb across my knee sending a chill up my spine. "If I see something, I like I try my hardest to get it." Two men started yelling in the front of the store and Eric sighed. "You can never have a moment of quiet in this town."

One of the men turned and glared at me. "You! What are you doing here?"

I looked at Eric's angry face to the man. "Me?"

The man snarled. "He bring you here to catch one of us for the vamps?! Huh? You think you can take me alive?!"

I shook my head. "I'm just eating ice cream I'm not doing anything."

Eric stood up slowly. "I think you both should leave."

The man took a step back. "You're not my alpha. You can't tell me what to do."

Eric smiled. "Would you like to settle this outside?"

The other man screamed. "Screw this!" I rolled out of my chair as he ran towards me and rolled to my feet in a loose ready stance. He snarled. "Oh you think you're tough?"

I shook my head. "No, not at all. I'm just trying to protect myself."

Eric jumped towards the man facing me and I ran out of the shop. It was cowardly, but I knew it was what Eric wanted. I had made it to the club when the second man finally caught me. He grabbed me around the neck and I knew I was sunk. His grip was too strong for human and he had been freaked about me being there. The man whispered, "Sweet dreams, Seer."

I closed my eyes and then the man's arm was gone. I opened my eyes slowly and found Jeremiah standing over the now limp body of the man. Jeremiah looked up at me and his eyes were golden bear's eyes. "Are you alright?"

I nodded. "Yes, but Eric was fighting another one at the ice cream shop."

Jeremiah picked me up in his arms and raced down the street much faster than a human could. We arrived at the ice cream shop to find Eric talking to a police officer who had the second man in handcuffs in the back of his car. Jeremiah set me down and Eric rushed over to me. "Are you alright?"

I nodded. "The other guy caught up to me, but Jeremiah saved me."

Eric looked up at Jeremiah and bowed his head slightly. "I'm in your debt it seems."

Jeremiah shook his head. "I would have protected her anyways. No male should harm a female. It's not natural."

Eric wrapped his fingers around mine. "Thank you."

I smiled at Jeremiah. "Yes, thank you."

Jeremiah smiled wide. "Anytime."

Eric led me back towards the club with Jeremiah walking in front of us. The man's body was gone by the time we got there and I felt a cold wind pass over me at the realization of how close I had come to dying. Eric led me passed the club and towards my house. I stopped him. "Eric, I can't…"

Eric shook his head. "Ciara I won't sleep well unless I know you're safe. Let me walk you home. Please."

I shook my head. "I wasn't going to say that. I was going to say I can't see you. It's too dangerous."

Eric pulled me against him and kissed my lips hard. My hands found their way to his back and I gripped his shirt. He pulled back and looked in to my eyes. "I'm sorry I let that one get away from me. I should have protected you. I won't let it happen again."

I wiped the tears that had magically appeared on my face. "I don't want you to get hurt. If anything…"

Eric kissed my lips softly. "If anything happens to you because I wasn't there, I won't be able to forgive myself. Can't you see how much I care about you?"

I leaned my head against his chest inhaling his scent deeply through my nose. "You're so stubborn."

He whispered, "It's what makes me a great attorney. Come on, let's get you home."

SIX

As soon as Eric left, I changed clothes, packed my backpack and walked to Akio's. His doors were closed so I knocked. I could hear him shuffling and then the door finally opened. He looked up at my face and smiled. "I told you so."

I rolled my eyes. "Hello to you too." I walked in to the dojo and set my bag down. "I need you to teach me. Somehow other beings know what I am. I don't know if one found out and told them or what, but they all keep calling me, Seer."

Akio shook his head. "I knew this would happen. We must train you to open it again before they come for you."

I frowned, "Come for me? Who's coming for me?"

Akio shook his head. "No time. Train." He barked orders at me and I followed them.

Five hours of training and then it finally opened. I gasped, "It's open. I can see all of your faces."

Akio frowned. "Which ones?"

I smiled and said. "Human, dragon, and tiger."

He nodded. "Good, now close it."

I groaned, but focused and it worked. I nodded then

focused and it opened. Akio sighed. "Good, now listen to me. There have been rumors that a group of vampires have come to this area in search of someone. I don't know for sure that it is you that they are looking for, but even if it is not they may still come for you. I want you to stay home and not go out. Okay?"

I nodded and bowed to him. "Thank you Master."

He nodded. "Call tomorrow and I will say if you come or not."

I nodded and grabbed my bag. Once I was outside, I let out a sigh. It was four thirty and the sun would be going down around six. I jogged home ignoring the pain in my legs and head and locked the door and checked all of the other locks. I pulled out the three stakes I kept in my house and set them around the house for easy access if a vampire somehow got in without my invitation, then changed and showered.

As I walked down the stairs, someone knocked on the front door. I continued slowly to the door and peeked through the peephole.

Eric.

I unlocked the doors and he came inside carrying two bags from the local sandwich shop. I slammed the door shut behind him and locked the doors. He walked ahead of me and got to the living room before I could. He stared down at the coffee table where a stake was sitting. "Expecting someone?" he asked with a curious twinkle in his eyes.

"I can't really explain…" I said as I fidgeted nervously. How does one explain that vampires and werewolves and everything that we are told are metaphors actually exist?

Eric set the food down and picked up one of the stakes. "Do you have any crosses?"

I shook my head then frowned. "Wait...you know about vampires?"

Eric smiled. "I know quite a bit."

I started to concentrate to open my eye, but Eric pulled me against him. "I won't let anyone hurt you. You know that right?"

I frowned. "Yeah, but..."

He shook his head. "Ciara, you're fired."

I stared at him in shock. "You're firing me? But I tried to quit and you wouldn't let me. Why are you firing me?"

He put his hand behind my neck and kissed my lips softly. "Because I can't date my secretary when she has an issue with dating her boss and I can't resist you anymore." I looked down, but he tilted my head back up. "Or was me being your boss just an easier excuse then telling me you aren't interested?"

I saw his guarded face and knew he expected me to hurt him. To deny my feelings for him.

I couldn't do it.

I pulled his head down and kissed him on the lips. He moaned as my tongue slipped across his lips, and he kissed me back as if I was air and he was suffocating. He picked me up and carried me to the couch.

I kissed him back as though he were the only thing keeping me alive.

He laid us down on the couch and ran his hand up and down the sides of my body as he kissed me.

I tugged at his shirt and he pulled back and took it off. I stared at his muscular upper chest and eight pack of abdominals. He was even sexier than I had imagined. I leaned up and kissed his ear and nibbled his neck. He moaned and nibbled my neck back. He pulled my shirt off and kissed down my chest and down my stomach. I gasped as he licked along my waistband. He sat back and stared at me smiling. I frowned. "What? What is it?"

He shook his head and lay down on top of me so that his eyes were level with mine. "I love you, Ciara."

I stared at him in shock then realized that as crazy as it was I felt the same. "I love you, too."

He smiled the most perfect smile I had ever seen and kissed me. He sat me up and was reaching around to unsnap my bra when the door splintered and broke open. Eric jumped up and stared at the door. "You do not have permission to enter this house."

I put my shirt back on and looked at the door. I opened my eye and stared in shock at the four men standing at my door, two of which were vampires and the other two werewolves.

I whispered to Eric, still watching the men, "Eric, two of them are werewolves. They don't need an invitation."

Eric growled beside me sounding like an animal. "I have claimed this woman as mine. You have no right to enter this house."

The vampires smiled. "You have not claimed her. She does not smell of you."

Eric sighed sadly. "Because you interrupted me. Come back in twenty minutes and let me finish."

I turned to look at Eric, shocked at what he said, and gasped as I saw a black furred wolf face with golden eyes overlapping Eric's human face. "You're...you're *not* human." I walked slowly back from him and he started to follow me.

"Ciara, I never lied to you."

I grabbed one of the stakes and shook my head. "No! Omission is as bad as lying! You should have told me."

He frowned and asked, "Would it have made a difference? Would you care any less for me?"

I shook my head and continued backing toward the side door. "You should have let me decide."

Eric groaned and threw his hands up into the air. "I thought you knew. You didn't tell me you weren't using your Sight. You are a Seer, so I thought you could See what I am. I thought you were just trying to get me to say it so you could refuse to see me."

I snarled. "It doesn't matter what I would have done you should have told me." The four at the door laughed and I glared at them. "What the hell do you want anyways?"

One of the vampires put his hand against the invisible barrier on the doorway. "If you let us in we could talk about it in a more civilized manner with you."

Eric growled. "No."

I glared at him. "My house." I turned to the vampire. "No. Tell me what you want."

The vampire said, "We are here to take you back to our Master. The Council wishes to start a force to find criminals who are in hiding and they feel that your particular talent would be most useful."

I folded my arms across my chest. "And what would I get to help them?"

Eric stared at me in complete shock. "You can't honestly be thinking about going with them? They'll just kill you as soon as you have worn out your use."

"I'm currently unemployed if you recall. And they'll just kill me if I refuse."

The vampire smiled. "She's very smart Eric. I can see why you want her."

Eric started toward them and I stepped between them and said, "Answer me vampire."

The vampire smiled. "You will be paid twice what you would make here, be provided with food and shelter and any thing else you require."

Eric shook his head. "Don't do it Ciara."

I spun on him and pushed him in the chest making him stumble. "Go in the kitchen. Let me talk to them."

He stared at me in shock. "If I am not here, they will send the wolves in to take you."

I growled in frustration. "I already have a wolf in here. Two more wouldn't make a difference."

Eric shook his head angrily. "You don't understand! I want to protect you. I wasn't lying about what I said."

"Just give me two minutes. If they try anything you can come try to kill them," I said with a smile.

He glared at the vampires and wolves and said, "If any of you touches a hair on her head I will kill you."

The wolves started to look nervous, buy nodded, and the vampires made an "X" over their hearts. Eric kissed me on the lips before I could pull away and stomped to the kitchen. I walked closer to the vampires and asked, "What's the real deal? What aren't you telling me?"

The other vampire smiled, "I can see that you are very smart and will be very helpful." His smile faded and he turned serious, "If you refuse our offer, we have been authorized to kill Eric and take you by force. A Seer like you cannot be without the protection of the Council or you will be killed by criminal preternaturals."

I stared at them in shock. "You'll kill Eric if I don't agree to come with you?"

The vampire nodded. "We do not want to, but our Master

was very specific that we use any negotiation technique necessary to get you to come with us."

I groaned. "Will you give me your word that if I join this force and help you that I will not be forced to change?"

The vampire smiled. "We would not try to change you anyways. You might lose your gift."

I looked toward the kitchen where I could hear Eric breaking plates. "You must promise not to hurt him. If you hurt him or kill him, I'll kill myself."

The werewolves stared at me in shock. The one on the right who looked to be the youngest asked, "You would give your life for his even though you shunned him for being a wolf?"

I sighed in frustration. "I didn't shun him because he is a wolf. I am angry with him because he didn't tell me. Plus, I love him and I don't want him hurt."

The first vampire said, "We need your answer."

I looked toward the kitchen and felt my longing for Eric. I did love him and I couldn't let him die. "I will join your force if none harm Eric, pay me what you said, feed me, give me housing and any other reasonable desire."

The two vampires nodded and spoke in unison, "You have our word."

Eric walked out of the kitchen and dropped to his knees in front of me, "Ciara, I'm begging you to stay with me. I can defeat them!"

I felt the tears threatening to break free and shook my head, "I'm sorry Eric. I have to accept their offer."

Eric jumped to his feet and grabbed my arms, "You don't know what you're saying! You can't trust them."

I looked up in to his eyes and saw his pain and his anger, "I love you and always will, but I must go with them. It's the only way."

He growled, "It's not. I can protect you."

I kissed his lips then quickly took off the ring handing it to him, "Move on Eric. Find another mate."

He shook his head and hugged me tight, "You're my mate. I only want you."

I shook my head and pulled out of his arms, "I'm sorry. You'll find another mate. I'm sorry." I backed up until I was outside the door and one of the vampires held out his hand.

Eric's body started shaking as he began the change, "I won't let them take you. You're mine! We belong together."

The two werewolves started moving toward him and I yelled, "You promised!"

The vampires hissed at the werewolves and they stopped. The vampire holding my hand picked me up in his arms and they ran. I could hear Eric's heartbroken howl behind us and cried in to the vampire's shirt. One of the werewolves barked and the vampire holding me sighed, "Just distract him until we are far enough away, but do not harm him. If you harm him, I will let Ciara kill you."

The werewolf barked again then disappeared. The vampire sighed and rubbed my cheek, "It will be all right. You will adapt to your new life and will be treated as royalty."

I stopped listening to his voice and focused instead on the sound of the wind rushing around us as we ran. The vampires climbed in to a black limousine and we drove away from Luna Villa. I hadn't even gotten to say goodbye to Akio. I knew Eric would find him and Akio would disown me. I would not be allowed to return and I would never be allowed to see Eric again.

I needed to focus on my new life and most importantly

keeping myself alive. I didn't want to be ruled by vampires, but if I worked for them and kept my head down then maybe I could adapt and live a life as normal as a Seer like me could have.

I curled up in to as small of a ball as I could in the limo and cried myself to sleep. I had a new life ahead of me and I would only allow this one cry over my former life and my one love. I would never love another man again.

Never.

THE STORY CONTINUES...

Continue Ciara's story in BARBARIC TENDENCIES

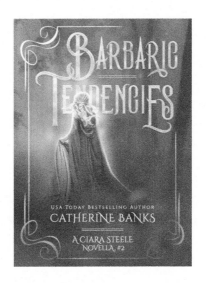

PREVIEW OF BARBARIC TENDENCIES

Here is a preview of Barbaric Tendencies (A Ciara Steele Novella #2)

Three weeks of training and I was already much better at fighting. I rolled to the side as my opponent slashed at me with his sword. The air whizzed by my head as I rolled again to dodge another strike. I grabbed the sword I had dropped earlier and blocked his sword from splitting my head. His blond hair was cropped in a military style buzz and glistened from the overhead lights. His teeth were gritted in concentration as he tried not to kill me, but still work me out. I got my legs under me and pushed up knocking him backwards. His handsome face brightened as he smiled and his blue eyes sparkled with delight as I pressed the tip of my sword against his throat. "Yield?" I asked breathlessly.

He swung his sword down and knocked my legs out from under me then pressed the tip of his sword to my throat. "Never."

I groaned and tossed my sword. "Dammit."

He sheathed his sword and extended his hand. "You're better, but I still don't know what the Council is thinking, sending you out in the field. You wouldn't survive ten seconds if I used all of my strength against you."

I took his hand and let him help me up. My muscles were screaming in protest and I stared at the ground for a moment while I regained my balance. I stood up fully and smiled while I said, "Jared, you have to admit that I'm better."

Jared snorted and said, "A ten-year-old wereanimal could take you down."

I rolled my eyes. "Wereanimals don't change until their sixteen and don't have the extra strength until then and you know it."

Jared winked one eye at me. "Exactly."

I pushed his chest and retrieved my sword from the ground. "Stupid tiger."

Jared snarled. "I heard that."

I set the sword in its rack. "You hear everything." I walked behind Jared as we headed to the mess hall. It seemed like years had passed since I had started my new life at the compound instead of the two months that it really was. A handsome man's face I was trying to forget flashed in front of my eyes wrenching my heart and making me stop walking. I leaned against the stone wall for support.

ABOUT THE AUTHOR

Catherine Banks is a USA Today bestselling fantasy author who writes in several fantasy subgenres and has multiple pseudonyms. She began writing fiction at only four years old and finished her first full-length novel at the age of fifteen. She is married to her soulmate and best friend, Avery, who she has two amazing children with. After her full-time job, she reads books, plays video games, and watches anime shows and movies with her family to relax. Although she has lived in Northern California her entire life, she dreams of traveling around the world. Catherine is also C.E.O. of Turbo Kitten Industries™, a company with many hats including being a book publisher and Etsy store full of nerdy fun.

facebook.com/catherinebanksauthor

twitter.com/catherineebanks

amazon.com/author/catherinebanks

bookbub.com/authors/catherine-banks

MORE FROM CATHERINE BANKS

YOUNG ADULT PARANORMAL & FANTASY ROMANCE SERIES

Artemis Lupine Series
Song of the Moon
Kiss of a Star
Healed by the Fire
Battles of the Night
Artemis Lupine, The Complete Series

Pirate Princess Series
Pirate Princess
Princess Triumvirate

Little Death Bringer Duology
Mercenary
Protector
Little Death Bringer, The Official Coloring Book

ADULT PARANORMAL & FANTASY ROMANCE SERIES

Zodiac Shifters Paranormal Romance Series

Centaur's Prize

Tiger Tears

Lion About

Ciara Steele Novella Series

True Faces

Barbaric Tendencies

ADULT REVERSE HAREM PARANORMAL & FANTASY ROMANCE SERIES

Her Royal Harem Series

Royally Entangled

Royally Exposed

Royally Elected

Royally Enraged

Her Royal Harem, The Complete Series

The Demon's Fair

Her Royal Harem, The Coloring Book

Wings of Vengeance Series

Of Dragons and Cruelty

Of Minotaurs and Sacrifice

Wings of Vengeance, The Complete Series

Anderelle: Minloa Trilogy

Queen of the Stars

Empress of the Galaxy

Goddess of the Universe

Anderelle: Minloa, The Complete Series

Bonds of Madness Series

Sealing the Deal

Her Super Harem Series

Lucky Strike

MORE FROM CATHERINE BANKS

STANDALONE CHILDREN'S BOOKS
Calvin's Alien Adventure

STANDALONE YOUNG ADULT PARANORMAL & FANTASY ROMANCE BOOKS
Monster Academy
Daughter of Lions
Lady Serra and the Draconian
Of Sky and Sea
The Last Werewolf
Sybil Deceived

STANDALONE ADULT PARANORMAL & FANTASY ROMANCE BOOKS
Dragon's Blood
Last Ama Princess
Transforming Rose
Alys of Asgard

Phoenix Possessed
Stone Heart

STANDALONE URBAN FANTASY BOOKS
The Pawn

ALSO BY CATHERINE BANKS

Books by **Kitten Wallace**

PanDora's Destruction

Deceived by the Alpha

Asgardian Mortal

Books by **Daisy Emory**

The Boyfriend Deal

Their Purple Girl

Made in the USA
Monee, IL
08 December 2020

51736576R00059